An Egg Is An Egg

written and illustrated by

NICKI WEISS

PAPERSTAR

The Putnam & Grosset Group

Copyright © 1990 by Monica J. Weiss. All rights reserved.
This book, or parts thereof, may not be reproduced in any form
without permission in writing from the publisher.
A PaperStar Book, published in 1996 by The Putnam & Grosset Group,
200 Madison Avenue, New York, NY 10016. PaperStar Books
and the PaperStar logo are trademarks of The Putnam Berkley Group, Inc.
Originally published in 1990 by G. P. Putnam's Sons, New York.
Published simultaneously in Canada.
Printed in the United States of America

Library of Congress Cataloging-in-Publication Data
Weiss, Nicki. An egg is an egg / Nicki Weiss. p.   cm.
Summary: A poetic explanation of how everything changes—eggs
to chicks, branches to sticks, green to white, and day to night.
[1. Change—Fiction. 2. Stories in rhyme.]   I. Title.
PZ8.3.W425Eg   1990   [E]—dc20   89-8462   CIP   AC
ISBN 0-698-11398-5
1   3   5   7   9   10   8   6   4   2

For Rachel

An egg is an egg
Until it hatches.

And then it is a chick.

A branch is a branch
Until it breaks.

And then it is a stick.

Nothing stays the same.
Everything can change.

A seed is a seed
Until it is sown.

And then it is a flower.

A block is a block
Until there are many.

And then they become a tower.

Nothing stays the same.
Everything can change.

Water is water
Until it is brewed.

And then it becomes tea.

You are you
Until I come.

And then you become "we."

Nothing stays the same.
Everything can change.

The yard is green
Until it snows.

And then it becomes white.

Day is day
Until sunset.

And then it is the night.

Nothing stays the same.
Everything can change.

This baby was a baby
Until he grew.

And now he is a boy.

But you can always be a baby.

You will always be my baby....

Some things stay the same.
Some things never change.
We Love you, Ben.